BEDTIME FAVORITES

DISNEY PRESS

New York

TABLE OF CONTENTS

SUSTAINABLE FORESTRY INITIATIVE

Certified Sourcing

www.sfiprogram.org

SFI-00993

For Text Only

The Big Campout

"Guess what?" Bonnie looked excitedly at her toys. "We're doing something really special tonight."

The toys were carefully arranged on Bonnie's bed. They couldn't wait to find out what the special something was. But they stayed motionless.

The little girl clapped her hands. "We're going on an adventure!"

The toys were excited, but they still didn't move.

"And we *all* get to go," Bonnie said. She carefully placed Woody, Buzz Lightyear, Slinky Dog, and all her new toys in a big tote bag. Next she collected her beloved old toys— Buttercup the unicorn, Trixie the triceratops, and a hedgehog called Mr. Pricklepants. A rag doll named Dolly came, too.

"We're going to have so much fun!" Bonnie told them.

Bonnie ran off to find a flashlight. Once she had left, all the toys suddenly came to life.

"I wonder where we're going," Mr. Pricklepants said.

"I hope there aren't any scary animals!" Rex the dinosaur whispered.

"I'll protect you," Woody the cowboy said with a wink.

Then the toys heard footsteps and stopped talking.

"We're camping out!" Bonnie announced happily as she came into the room. She scooped up the tote bag.

A few minutes later, Bonnie and her toys were in the backyard. "Here we are!" she said. Bonnie carefully unpacked the toys and began arranging them inside a tent she had set up. "You sit next to Trixie," she told Rex, placing the two dinosaurs side by side. "Buttercup, Woody, and Buzz, you guys will be next to my sleeping bag." Soon everyone had their own spot.

"Now let's have a picnic!" Bonnie began passing out toy food and toy plates. "Corn for Buttercup, pepperoni pizza for Rex, spaghetti for Bullseye—"

"Bonnie! Dinnertime!" a voice called out. It was Bonnie's mother.

Bonnie giggled. "I've got to go eat *my* dinner. But don't worry— I'll be back soon." She gave each toy a hug, then crawled out of the tent.

Left alone in the tent, the toys began to explore.

"This is a right comfortable spot," Jessie said, admiring Bonnie's puffy sleeping bag.

"The accommodations really *are* quite satisfactory," Mr. Pricklepants agreed.

"Well, shine my spurs!" Woody exclaimed, noticing an electric

camping lantern. He turned it on, and a warm glow lit up the tent. He motioned for the toys to gather in a circle.

"Let's have a sing-along," Woody suggested. He held his cowboy hat over his heart and began to sing "Camptown Races."

Jessie quickly joined in, and Bullseye stomped his hooves in time to the beat. The other toys began singing, too.

After a few more songs, the toys went outside. They still had some time before Bonnie returned, and they wanted to explore.

Mr. Potato Head peeked through the tent flaps. It had gotten dark. "The coast is clear."

The toys stepped into the backyard.

"Look!" Buttercup said. "The stars are coming out!"

Buzz smiled. "That, my friend, is the Big Dipper—seven stars that form a ladle shape." He pointed toward the constellation.

"You sure know a lot about the sky," Trixie said, impressed.

Buzz grinned. "Comes with the space-ranger territory."

"I just saw a shooting star!" Mr. Potato Head shouted.

"I think that was a firefly," Hamm said.

Jessie hopped on Bullseye. "I'm going to explore the yard!"

Buttercup trotted over. "Follow me! I'll show you the rose bed near the sprinklers."

Trixie turned to the other toys. "Who wants to play freeze tag?" But before anyone could answer, she tapped Rex. "Tag. You're frozen!"

Smiling, the rest of the toys began running away as Trixie chased after them.

"The flower bed is out-of-bounds!" she shouted.

"Hey! Someone? Tag me?" Rex called, still frozen. "Anyone?"

"I'm wiped out," Hamm said a little while later.

"How about a shadow-puppet production?" suggested Mr. Pricklepants.

"Good idea," Woody said, leading the toys into the tent. "Bonnie's going to be back soon."

The toys used Bonnie's flashlight to create shadow puppets on the tent. Buzz made an airplane with his wings. Mr. Pricklepants made an elephant.

Rex peeked outside the tent window. "Boy, it sure got dark fast," he remarked.

Then Dolly made a pair of bunny ears behind his head. Everyone laughed, even Rex.

"A sleepover wouldn't be complete without a scary story," Mr. Potato Head said. He clicked off the flashlight so the toys would be in darkness. "Once there was a little toy that got lost in the forest. The forest was dark. Very dark."

"Just like now!" Rex exclaimed, beginning to get scared.

"Suddenly there were footsteps," Mr. Potato Head said.

The toys heard the sound of someone running.

"Like now!" Jessie said with a gasp.

Mr. Potato Head continued his story. "A monster was coming—"

"*Aaah!*" Rex shrieked as a huge shadow loomed over the tent.

The toys all flopped down and went still.

The tent flap opened. . . .

"I'm back!" Bonnie said, smiling at her toys.

She brought the toys outside and placed them in a circle around the lantern. She gave each one a marshmallow on a twig. "It wouldn't be a campout if we didn't toast marshmallows!" she announced happily.

The toys couldn't have agreed more. And Rex was especially glad that there wasn't a real monster after all!

THE LION KING

Simba's Big Secret

Simba and Nala were best friends. The lion cubs did just about everything together. They splashed in the water hole, snuck up on bugs, and raced through the high grass. They liked to tell each other secrets, too.

"I'm a little scared of mice," Nala told Simba one day. "Don't tell anybody."

"Don't worry, I won't," Simba said. "I get scared of the dark sometimes."

"Your secret is safe with me," said Nala.

Simba smiled at her. "Thanks," he said. "You're a good friend."

One day, Simba and his father, Mufasa, were out for a walk.

"Look at that little mouse stuffing her cheeks with seeds," said Mufasa.

"That's so funny!" said Simba. "I don't know why Nala's scared of mice."

"I remember when I was a cub. I was scared of mice, too!" Mufasa said with a chuckle.

Nala was just on the other side of the hill, chasing butterflies. She heard Simba talking with his dad, and she got really mad.

Later, Nala went to find Simba.

"You promised not to tell my secret!" she told him angrily. "And now your father knows. He'll tell everybody, and they'll all laugh at me! That's the last time I'm going to trust you."

"I'm sorry, Nala! Please don't stop trusting me!" Simba

pleaded. "I'll never tell anyone else what you say, I promise."

"Well . . ." said Nala, "we'll see."

Nala didn't stop playing with Simba, but she did stop telling him secrets.

A few weeks later, Nala finally changed her mind.

"I'm going to tell you a secret," she said to Simba, "but it's a really big one. If you tell this time, I'll be so mad at you I won't be your friend anymore."

"I promise I won't say anything!" said Simba.

"Okay," said Nala. "Here's the secret: I found a huge cave yesterday, down in the red cliffs. But I was with my mother, so I couldn't go in. I'm going back to explore it today."

"Can I come with you?" Simba asked.

"No, I want to go by myself," she replied as she walked away. "Maybe you can come some other day."

Simba played all day without Nala. A little before dinner, he began to wonder when she was coming back.

Nala's mother was worried. "Simba," she asked, "do you have any idea where Nala is? Did she mention anything to you about going somewhere new or different?"

"No," he answered. He could not look her in the eye. It was the first time he had not told a grown-up the truth. But he'd made a promise to Nala, and he didn't want to break it.

The sun went down and the moon shone in the sky. Nala's mother paced back and forth. "Where can she be?" she kept asking.

Simba wished he could tell her.

A couple of hours later, Nala still hadn't returned. The whole pride was worried about her.

Sarabi, Simba's mother, went to her son. "Do you know where Nala is?" she asked.

"I can't tell," said Simba. "It's a secret."

"A secret? What kind of a secret?" his mother asked.

"A big secret. I can't tell, no matter what!" he cried, explaining how mad Nala had been when he'd told Mufasa she was afraid of mice.

"Simba," said his mother, "you're a good friend to try not to tell Nala's secret. But there are some secrets that are good to keep and others that are important to tell."

"How do you know the difference?" asked Simba.

"If you think about it," Sarabi replied, "you will know in your heart if something is a good secret or a bad secret. Nala could be in trouble."

Simba thought about what his mother had said. He decided that he had to tell everyone where Nala was.

He pointed to the red cliffs. "She's over there," Simba said, "in a cave."

Sarabi hugged her son. "That was the right thing to do. Now, let's go find Nala."

The whole pride hurried across the grasslands. "Nala!" called her mother.

"*Naaalaa!*" Simba yelled.

There was only silence.

"Nala!" her mother called again.

Then, at last, they heard a small voice. "M-mother?" It was Nala!

The lions rushed to where the voice had come from. It was the entrance to a cave, but it was almost completely blocked. A rock slide had trapped the little cub!

The lions dug and dug, and finally they cleared the rocks away.

Nala rushed out of the cave and ran to her mother.

"Nala! I was so worried about you!" her mother cried.

"I'm sorry!" said Nala. "I was so scared! I'll never go anywhere without telling you again."

A few minutes later, Simba walked over to his friend and hung his head. "I'm sorry I told your secret, Nala," he said. "Please don't be too mad at me."

"Why would I be mad at you?" said Nala. "If you hadn't said anything, I would still be trapped."

When they got home, it was time for bed. "I'm so happy to be back!" Nala exclaimed.

"Me, too," said Simba. "And that's not a secret!"

Nala smiled. She and Simba drifted off to sleep, dreaming of their next adventure together.

The Secret Adventure

Early one morning, Thumper hopped over to a thicket. "Bambi, Bambi, wake up!" the bunny whispered to the sleeping fawn.

Bambi stirred and gave a great big yawn. "Mmmm, I'll be right there," he mumbled. He stood up sleepily. "I have to tell my mother where we're going."

"You can't do that," Thumper said. "It's a secret. Besides, she'd never let us go."

The friends hopped off to find Flower.

A few minutes later, Bambi and Thumper spotted their skunk friend. "Good morning, Flower," they said.

"Thumper wants to go on a secret adventure," Bambi said. "Do you want to come along?"

"Oh, gosh! I do," Flower said shyly. "But would you tell me what we're doing?"

Bambi looked at Thumper eagerly. He wanted to know, too.

Thumper puffed up his chest and said proudly, "I want to show you what the beavers build on water!"

Bambi and Flower looked at each other. They didn't understand how anyone could build something on water. But it sure sounded exciting.

The three friends didn't notice a red bird perched on a branch above them.

The bird was a friend of Bambi's mother. He flew to her and told her where the young prince was headed.

"Maybe it would be good for Bambi and his friends to explore the forest on their own," Bambi's mother told the bird, whose name was Red. "Would you mind keeping an eye on them?"

Red agreed and then flew off to tell Thumper's mother.

Meanwhile, Thumper and Flower were hard at work, trying to push Bambi through a tight thicket. He was stuck!

"Why are we going this way?" Bambi asked.

"Shhh!" Thumper whispered. "We can't go the regular way. We are really close to the meadow where all the bunnies graze—including my mama," he explained quietly. "If she sees us, she'll say I have to look after my silly sisters!"

Suddenly some branches gave way and the three friends fell out onto the meadow.

Bambi, Thumper, and Flower quickly ran back into the bushes. They peeked out to see if the bunnies had spotted them.

"No one is looking at us," Thumper said. "My mama is talking with her friend Red. I think we're safe. Come on, let's go!"

But they had been spotted! Thumper's sisters had seen everything. They wanted to know what their big brother was up to, so they followed him. So did Red.

The three friends continued walking through the woods. Soon they came to a stream. Thumper looked around. He was not sure where to go next.

Suddenly, a beaver with big teeth and a large, flat tail walked up to them. "Who are you?" Bambi asked.

"My name is Slap," the beaver said. "Where are you going?"

Thumper hopped forward. "I wanted to show my friends what the beavers build on the river," he explained.

"We call it a dam," said Slap, "and I can show you the way."

A little while later, they arrived at the dam.

"Here we are," Slap said proudly. Everywhere along the river, the beavers were busy. Some were in the water pushing logs, while others were chopping down trees with their strong teeth.

"Come out onto the dam," Slap offered.

Thumper and Flower went first and Bambi followed, a bit unstable on his legs. Soon they were balancing on  the logs among the working beavers.

"Hey, this is fun!" Thumper shouted.

"Why do they call you Slap?" Flower asked their new beaver friend shyly.

"I'll show you," Slap replied. He started slapping the logs with his flat tail. "I'm the best slapper in the whole river!" he exclaimed.

The dam shook and shook when the beaver was slapping.

"Help! Help, Thumper!" four little voices suddenly cried.

It was Thumper's younger sisters! They had gone out on the dam as it started to shake. Now the log they were sitting on was floating away!

"Oh, no! My sisters!" Thumper exclaimed. "We have to rescue them!"

"Hurry—they are headed toward the waterfall!" Slap shouted.

All the beavers jumped into the water and quickly swam toward the log. High above, Red flew off to tell Mama Bunny and Bambi's mother.

Thumper's sisters held on to each other and tried to balance so they would not fall into the river. But they were getting close to the waterfall!

A few minutes later, Slap and the two other beavers reached the runaway log. They slapped their tails with all their might, and slowly but surely, they got the log to the riverbank.

Bambi stood in the water with Thumper perched on his head. One by one, Thumper pulled his sisters to safety.

Once everyone was back on land, Thumper thanked the beavers for their bravery.

"You're welcome," said Slap. "Can you find your way home from here?"

"Nothing to it," Thumper said. "We live just around that thicket, and to the right."

Thumper began to lead the others through the woods. But he couldn't seem to find the path home, so they kept walking and walking.

After a while, it began to get dark.
The trees blocked the light from the
fading sun, and the branches swayed,
casting scary shadows all around.

"Uh, Thumper," Bambi said, "I
think we might be lost."

"Oh, don't be silly," Thumper
said, looking back at his friends. "It's
just like in the daytime . . . only darker.
There's nothing to be afraid of here—especially
when you're with the bravest rabbit in the forest!"

Suddenly Thumper hopped into something. *"Aaaahhh!"* he
screamed.

Luckily it was not a monster that Thumper had run into.
It was his own mother! She and Bambi's mother had finally
found them.

"Oh, I'm so glad you are safe!" cried Bambi's mother as she led them into the meadow, where there was more sunlight. "Red was keeping an eye on you. He told us what happened."

Until now the friends had not noticed the bird, who was flitting in the air above them.

Thumper's mother tapped her foot angrily. "Thumper! What does your father always tell you?"

Thumper looked down at the ground. He didn't like to be scolded. "Never go off on your own without telling someone first," he replied.

"That's right," Thumper's mother said. "You all must promise never to do that again."

They all agreed, though Thumper didn't seem too happy about it.

"Good," said Bambi's mother. "Now let's go home. The sun has started to set."

Soon the group returned home.

"Good night, everyone," Flower said.

"Good night, Flower!" the others called.

"Good night, Bambi," Thumper said.

"Good night, Thumper," Bambi replied. Then he whispered, "Thanks for taking me on a secret adventure."

Thumper smiled. He and his family went to their burrow. Soon the bunny was fast asleep, dreaming of his next adventure.

Not far away, Bambi's eyelids fluttered shut. It had been a long and exciting day, and he was tired.

Moonlight beamed over the meadow, and everything in the forest was still and peaceful . . . at last.

Lilo & Stitch

Doggone It, Stitch!

Stitch, an alien who lived on Earth, was sitting in the living room waiting for his friend, Lilo, to come home from school. Just then, Lilo burst into the house carrying a puppy.

"Hi, Stitch!" Lilo said excitedly. "My neighbor Leilani asked me to take care of her puppy, Rover, while she visits her grandmother."

"Stitch wants to listen to music," Stitch said.

"Not now," Lilo answered. "I have to take care of Rover."

Stitch watched Lilo make a bed for Rover. He watched her scratch the dog's ears and rub his tummy. Stitch was bored. He wanted Lilo to play with him.

"Can we listen to music *now*?" Stitch asked.

"I want to teach Rover some new tricks," Lilo said. She showed the puppy how to roll over. Then she threw him a ball and gave him treats.

55

Lilo taught Rover tricks all afternoon while Stitch watched quietly. The dog learned to sit, to beg, and to stay.

"Way to go, Rover!" Lilo said encouragingly. "You're a good doggie!" She patted him on the head.

"Music, now?" Stitch asked again.

"Later," Lilo replied. "Rover's hungry."

That evening, Nani, Lilo's older sister, came home from work. She and Lilo watched Rover play tug-of-war with the kitchen rug. "Oh, isn't he cute!" Nani exclaimed. They laughed at everything Rover did. They didn't pay any attention to poor Stitch.

Stitch went upstairs. He felt a little sad. Maybe if I act like a puppy, he thought, Lilo will play with me. He flopped on the bed and went to sleep.

The next morning, Stitch tried to act like Rover. He hid Lilo's shoes and chewed the kitchen rug. But that only made Lilo angry.

"You need a time-out," she told Stitch. "Go to our room while I take Rover for a walk."

Stitch waited until Lilo and Rover had gone. Then he hurried outside and ran toward town.

When Lilo and Rover came home, it was time for Lilo to go to her hula class. Lilo couldn't find Stitch anywhere. She wondered why he wasn't home. Stitch loved dancing the hula.

I guess I'll have to go without him, Lilo thought.

Stitch still wasn't home when Lilo returned. Lilo asked Nani and her friend David if they had seen him.

Before they could answer, Cobra Bubbles called. He was a social worker Lilo and Nani knew.

"You need to hide Stitch," Cobra told Lilo. "Two scientists from the Center for the Study of Aliens are looking for him. They want to take him to their laboratory."

"But I don't know where Stitch is!" Lilo exclaimed. "He's gone!"

"Well, I suggest you find him before the scientists do," Cobra replied.

Lilo and Nani went to town to look for Stitch. David drove
to the beach to search.

"Stitch has been acting weird all day," Lilo told Nani. "His
badness level was way up. He hid my shoes and chewed the rug.
He acted just like Rover!"

Suddenly, Lilo knew where Stitch had gone. "Stitch probably thought I liked Rover better because he's a puppy. I bet Stitch went to the animal shelter to watch the puppies!" She grabbed Nani's hand and pulled her toward the shelter.

When Lilo and Nani arrived, Stitch was there.

"Stitch learning to be cute like puppy," he explained when he saw them. "So Lilo like him again."

"Stitch, I like you just the way you are," Lilo answered. "Now, let's go home!"

But when they started to leave, they saw the two scientists coming toward them. "Nani!" Lilo cried. "We've got to do something!"

Nani spotted two dust mops in the shelter closet. She tied the mops onto Stitch so he looked like a long-haired puppy.

Lilo put a leash on Stitch, and they walked slowly out of the shelter and past the scientists. The scientists watched Stitch suspiciously.

Just then, Cobra Bubbles and David drove up.

"Hey, scientists!" David called. "We just saw an alien heading out to sea. You'd better hurry if you want to catch it. Hop in, and we'll take you there."

The scientists jumped into the car, and Cobra Bubbles and David sped off.

Stitch was safe!

Lilo, Nani, and Stitch went home, where Rover was waiting patiently. Stitch went over to the dog and pointed to his paw.

"Stitch show you how to shake your paw," the alien said. Lilo smiled. She was happy Stitch wanted to make friends with Rover, but now it was time for the puppy to go home.

A few minutes later, David returned. "Cobra said the scientists are heading out to sea to look for Stitch. He's safe for now."

"And look what I found at the beach," he added. He lifted a kitten out of a bag and set her on the floor.

The kitten began to explore the room. After a few minutes, David left to go to work.

"How cute," Lilo said. Stitch watched everyone play with the kitten. Then the kitten spotted the alien and ran to him. Stitch scooped her up and gave her a big hug. The kitten was soft and cuddly. She began to purr.

Stitch found some string and began to play with the kitten. She darted this way and that, trying to grab the end as Stitch moved it around.

Then the alien took the kitten outside. "Stitch teach you tricks now," he said. He taught the kitten to come when he called and to stay in one spot.

Lilo watched from the window. "Stitch is really good at having a pet," she said.

Nani glanced outside. "Yes, he seems happy," she remarked.

After a while, it was time to eat. "Dinner!" Lilo called.

Instead of racing to the table as he usually did, Stitch got some food and fed the kitten first. Then he sat down and ate with Lilo and Nani.

After dinner, Stitch played with the kitten some more. But the kitten had had a long day. She soon climbed into Stitch's lap and fell asleep.

Lilo and Nani went into the kitchen to frost a cake that Nani had made earlier.

A few minutes later, Stitch joined them. "Can Stitch keep the kitten?" he asked.

"I think the kitten has already adopted you," Nani replied. "You're her family now."

"The cake says 'OHANA, STITCH,'" Lilo said. "And you know what that means."

Stitch nodded. "'*Ohana* means family—and that means nobody gets left behind."

Nani smiled. "Now let's eat some cake and go to bed. Tomorrow we have to show the kitten her new neighborhood."

Mickey Mouse and the Pet Shop

Mickey Mouse was a great friend of Mr. Palmer, the owner of the local pet shop. One day, Mr. Palmer had to go on an overnight trip. He couldn't leave the animals by themselves, so he asked Mickey to watch the shop while he was gone.

"I will be back tomorrow afternoon," said Mr. Palmer as he waved good-bye. "You shouldn't have any problems."

"Have a good time," called Mickey. "This will be a snap!"

"A snap!" a parrot repeated.

Mickey decided to get to know the animals. So he walked around, gazing at the colorful fish, talking parrots, furry kittens, and cuddly dogs. They all seemed content—except for a cute little puppy who wouldn't stop whimpering.

"Poor little fella," said Mickey. "What you need is some attention." He picked up the puppy.

The puppy wriggled out of Mickey's arms and raced over to the fishbowl for a drink of water.

"Watch out!" screeched the parrot. "Watch out!"

He was too late. The puppy knocked over the bowl, and the fish went flying across the store.

"Gotcha!" Mickey called as he caught the fish and put it in a new bowl. He put the puppy back in the kennel.

Just then, the door opened. It was Mickey's first customer! He was so excited that he forgot to lock the kennel door.

"Can I help you?" Mickey asked.

Before the woman could answer, the puppy had gotten out and opened the door to the mice's cage. Now mice were everywhere!

"*Oh, my!* I'll come back later—much later!" cried the woman as she raced for the door.

After the customer left, Mickey put the animals back where they belonged. This time he made sure he locked the doors.

"Don't worry, little guy," he said to the puppy. "Someone will come for you. You'll see." Then Mickey went upstairs for the night.

When Mickey tried to go to sleep, the puppy howled and howled. Mickey tried hiding under the covers, but that didn't work. He could still hear. Then he tried covering his ears with a pillow. That didn't work either. Mickey didn't know what to do.

Finally, the puppy got exactly what he wanted—a cozy spot under the covers, right next to Mickey!

When Mickey woke up the next morning, the puppy was gone. Mickey looked all over the house for him, but he was nowhere to be found. Maybe he's downstairs, thought Mickey.

Mickey couldn't believe his eyes when he walked into the pet shop. It was a mess! Books were scattered on the floor, and the plants had been turned over. But the puppy wasn't there.

Mickey got dressed and then began to look for his little friend. He was about to give up when he remembered to check the storage room. Sure enough, the puppy was there.

Mickey picked up the puppy, brought him back to the kennel, and locked the door. "Now you can't cause any more trouble."

"Well," said Mickey with a sigh. "I guess I should begin tidying up the store."

As he worked, the puppy began to whine. Mickey felt bad, so he opened the kennel door. The puppy followed him around, trying to be good.

He helped Mickey put the books back, dust the counter, and sweep up the soil from the flowerpots.

"You may be a rascal," said Mickey, "but I sure am getting used to having you around."

Mickey and the puppy had just finished cleaning up when Mr. Palmer strode in.

"It looks like everything went smoothly," he said. "I hope none of the animals gave you any trouble."

"It was as easy as pie," a very tired Mickey replied.

Then Mr. Palmer handed Mickey his paycheck. "Thanks for helping me out," he said. "I hope you will come back soon."

Mickey just smiled.

As Mickey was about to leave, the puppy began to howl.

"I'm going to miss you, too, little fella," Mickey said sadly.

Suddenly Mickey had an idea. He could take the pup instead of the pay! Now everybody would be happy—especially the parrot, who screeched, "And don't come back!"

"But what should I call you?" Mickey wondered aloud.

Just then, Mickey saw some pictures of outer space in a newspaper. The headline read: NEW PICTURES OF PLUTO! "That's it! I'll call you Pluto!" he exclaimed.

Pluto licked Mickey's cheek happily. From that day on, Mickey and Pluto were the best of friends.

Sleeping Beauty

A Lullaby for Fairies

One evening, Princess Aurora invited her fairy friends, Flora, Fauna, and Merryweather, to the castle. They had a lovely dinner and told stories. But the hours passed quickly, and soon it was time to go to bed.

"Let's have a good-night song," Fauna suggested.

"You mean a lullaby?" Aurora asked.

"Oh, that sounds lovely," Merryweather said.

So they sang and twirled each other around.

"Now it's really time for bed," Flora finally said, when each of them had sung once.

"Do we have to go to bed?" Fauna protested.

"I think it would be a good idea," Flora replied. "After all, we've got a lot to do tomorrow."

"You're right. Good night," said Aurora.

"Sleep tight," said the fairies.

Before long, everyone was fast asleep—except for Flora.
Poor Flora tossed and turned. She flipped and flopped. And
she accidentally bonked Merryweather right on the head!

"Ouch!" cried Merryweather. "Why did you wake me up?"

"I'm sorry," said Flora. "I can't fall asleep."

"Why don't you count sheep?" Fauna suggested.

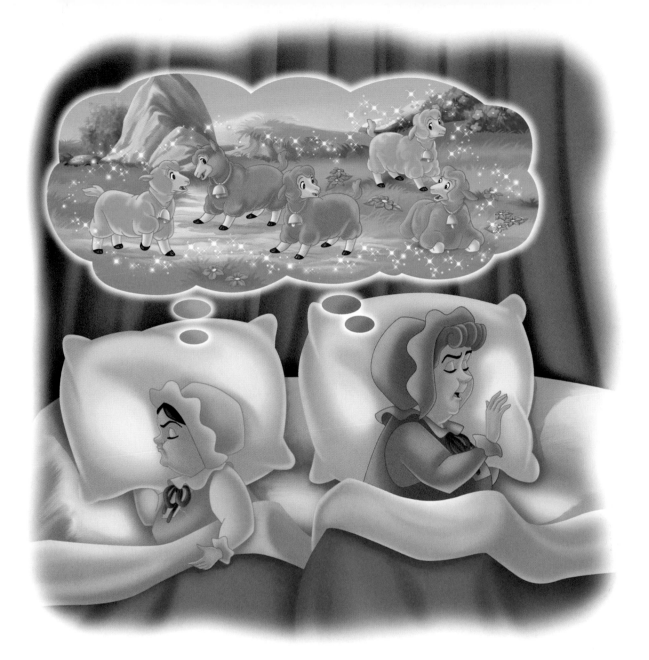

So the fairies started to count: "One, two, three . . ." The fairies counted louder and faster. ". . . thirty . . . forty . . . eighty-two . . . one hundred!" Sure enough, they woke Aurora.

"Will you two please keep it down?" pleaded Fauna. "The princess needs her sleep."

"Flora was supposed to count the blue sheep," said Merryweather.

"No, no, no," replied Flora. "I was supposed to count the *pink* sheep."

The fairies' voices got even louder as they argued.

The princess wanted to get everyone back to sleep before they woke the entire palace! So she started to sing a lullaby:

"The sun has set; it's time for bed.

Close your eyes and rest your head."

Aurora's soothing song calmed the fairies immediately. The sweet tune made their eyelids heavy. Soon they were all fast asleep—even Flora.

"Ah, sleep at last!" Aurora sighed happily. She continued to hum the lullaby as she settled back down under her blanket. And soon, the princess was fast asleep, too, dreaming about adventures with friends . . . and pink and blue sheep.

The Spooky Sleepover

It was a quiet morning at Monsters, Inc., and James P. Sullivan, also known as Sulley, was catching up on paperwork. He smiled as he reviewed the monthly laugh reports.

At Monsters, Inc., it was the monsters' job to go to the human world and make kids laugh. The laughs were used as energy for the city of Monstropolis. It had been Sulley's idea, and now he was president of Monsters, Inc. He was glad everything was going so well.

Suddenly, the phone rang. "Hello?" said Sulley.

"It's dispatch," said the voice on the other end of the line. "Annual slumber party at little Shannon Brown's house. Waxford is out sick. We need a replacement."

"I'll get right on it," replied Sulley. He knew that there would be lots of kids at the party, and he wanted to make sure he had a monster there to tell jokes and capture laughs.

Sulley thought about who to send. He wanted to put his best monster on the case. He smiled to himself. Who better for the job than his one-eyed pal, Mike Wazowski? Mike was Monsters, Inc.'s top Laugh Collector. He could make anyone laugh. Sulley knew his best friend would be perfect for the job.

Mike was in the locker room getting ready for work. He had just finished putting in his contact lens—which was the size of a pizza—when Sulley walked in. Sulley explained the situation.

"I'm your man," Mike said confidently.

"Great!" Sulley exclaimed. Whistling, he went back to his office to finish his laugh reports.

"Piece of cake," Mike said as a door slid into his station on the Laugh Floor. "One joke and I'll collect enough energy for the year!" Then Mike opened the door and walked through the closet in Shannon Brown's room. It was empty.

"Uh . . . hello?" Mike called. He looked around the room. He peeked under the bed—but there was no one there. Some party, he thought. I wonder where everyone is. Maybe I should go back. Just as Mike started walking toward the closet, he heard the sound of laughter.

"All right, now we are in business!" Mike exclaimed. "Kids, prepare to laugh."

Just then, thunder cracked across the sky, and a flash of lightning lit up the dark room. Mike jumped. If there was one thing he didn't like, it was a thunderstorm.

"I'm okay! I'm fine!" Mike shouted. Then he ran to the closet door to return to the factory.

Mike jiggled the doorknob, but it just opened into the closet, not the Laugh Floor at Monsters, Inc. There was no way out.

Mike soon realized that lightning must have struck the door and broken it. "Don't panic, don't panic," he told himself, his voice shaking. He knew he had to find the slumber party and another closet door—fast. Otherwise, who knew how long he'd be stuck there?

Mike took a deep breath and headed into the dark hallway. He was sure he heard laughter coming from somewhere. Now all he had to do was find it. As he started walking, the floor made a noise beneath him. *Crrreeaak!*

Halfway down the hallway, Mike stopped and looked around. There were some paintings on the wall that looked very creepy. They gave Mike goose bumps. He was pretty sure the people in the paintings were staring right at him! "I've got to get out of here," Mike muttered to himself as he continued down the hallway. Then he saw something and froze.

Mike couldn't believe his eye. Sitting at the end of the hall was a large furry creature with fangs. It was panting heavily.

"Oh, man!" he cried. "Am I ever glad to see a fellow monster around here."

Taking a deep breath, Mike started to walk closer to the creature. Just as he did, the creature knocked him down.

"Ahhhhhhhhhhh!" Mike screamed. "Dog breath!" Mike hated dogs!

He pushed the dog off him and ran as fast as he could into a nearby room. He slammed the door shut. He was safe—for now!

Meanwhile, back at Monsters, Inc., Sulley was working on the Laugh Floor. The floor manager came running over. "Sulley! Sulley!" he shouted. "Mike still hasn't returned from the slumber party. He's never been gone this long!"

When Sulley went to check on the door, he discovered it wasn't working. That meant Mike was trapped in Shannon Brown's house!

"Uh-oh," said Sulley. "We've got to get Mike out of that closet. I can't believe he's stuck!"

Sulley brought in a maintenance crew to figure out how to fix the door.

Together the monsters pulled all the levers and pushed all the buttons on the door to try and get it to open properly.

When that didn't work, Sulley read the emergency manuals. He and the other monsters tried everything they could. After a few hours, the door made a clicking sound. It was working! Now it would open into a different room at Shannon's house. The monsters cheered.

Back in the house, Mike walked into the bathroom.

"Ouch!" the green monster squealed as he tripped on a yellow rubber ducky and went rolling across the floor. Finally, Mike crashed into the wall and stopped. Then he heard a lot of giggling from down the hall.

Mike did not like this assignment—or this house—but he was determined to find the party. So he lifted himself off the floor and followed the laughter. But when he found the right door and opened it, it was quiet.

Slowly, Mike entered the dark, silent room. All of a sudden, a light went on! Mike jumped. Shannon Brown and all her friends started roaring with laughter! They thought Mike looked funny sneaking into the room.

"Ahhhhhhhh!"

Mike was so
frightened that
he couldn't stop
yelling.

At that exact
moment, the closet
door opened, and
Sulley burst into
the room. When
he heard Mike, he
started screaming, too. Then he and Mike jumped toward each
other and huddled together.

The girls at the slumber party laughed and laughed. A big
blue monster with purple spots hugging a one-eyed little green
monster was one of the funniest things they had ever seen.

112

Mike and Sulley looked at each other and smiled. Then Mike jumped to the floor, and they both took a bow. The kids cheered.

"Looks as if our work here is done," Sulley said. He and Mike headed through the closet door and back to the Monsters, Inc. Laugh Floor. They had filled so many canisters with laughs that Mike was named the top Laugh Collector that day.

"I was never scared for a second," said Mike, hoping Sulley would believe him.

"Me neither, buddy," Sulley replied, his big furry fingers crossed behind his back. "Me neither."

Cinderella
Bedtime for Gus

Cinderella looked out her bedroom window as the sun was setting over the horizon. The sky was golden and orange. In the distance, the clock in the tower of the castle read eight o'clock.

Cinderella leaned over and tapped gently on the walls of her attic room. "Bedtime, everyone!" she called.

Jaq, Suzy, Gus, and the other mice hurried out of their mouse hole. Cinderella did all of the household chores in her wicked stepmother's house. She never had time for fun, so the birds and mice were her only friends.

"Bedtime already?" Jaq cried.

"Buh-bedtime?" Gus asked. Gus was Cinderella's newest mouse friend. She had just rescued him from a trap that morning.

"Bedtime, Gus-Gus," Suzy explained. "Close eyes and . . . zzzz . . . fall asleep!"

Gus looked confused. He closed his eyes and started to tip over.

Jaq caught him. "Not *fall*, Gus-Gus," he said. "Fall asleep. Like this." He put his head on his hands and pretended to snore.

Cinderella laughed. "Falling asleep isn't all there is to bedtime," she said. "Gus has never lived in a house before. We'll have to teach him about getting ready for bed."

"Okay! Okay!" the other mice cried. "Show Gus-Gus!"

"First," Cinderella said, "you have to put on your pajamas."

She went to her dresser and pulled out a tiny pair of striped pajamas for Gus. "Here, try these on."

Soon all the mice were in their pajamas. Gus even wore a pair of cozy slippers.

"That's better," Cinderella declared. "Pajamas are much more comfortable for sleeping than regular clothes."

Gus nodded. "Gus-Gus *loves* pajamas!" he exclaimed. "Gus-Gus wears pajamas all the time!"

Cinderella smiled. "I'm glad you like your pajamas Gus, but they are only for while you're sleeping."

The mouse nodded.

"Now sleep, Cinderella?" another mouse cried.

Cinderella smiled. "Not quite yet," she said to the young mouse. "First, wash your faces and brush your teeth. When you're all scrubbed and brushed, I'll kiss you good night, and then Suzy will tuck everyone in."

The mice began to brush their teeth. "Mmm-mmm," Gus said with a smile, tasting the minty toothpaste.

The other mice giggled and finished up. Gus watched carefully, and before long, he was done, too.

"Tuh-tuck in?" Gus
asked.

Jaq pulled him
toward the washbasin.
"Not yet, Gus-Gus,"
he said. He handed
him some soap.

Gus watched as
the other mice washed

their faces with tiny cloths and patted themselves dry with old
rags. Then he did the same.

When the mice were all neat and clean, Cinderella kissed
them good night. "It's time for everyone to go to sleep."

"Follow me," Jaq told Gus. He ran over to his little bed and
hopped in. The he pointed to the bed next to him. "That's your
bed," he said. Gus grinned and got under the covers.

Suzy tucked in each of the mice.

"Story, Cinderelly!" the mice cried. "Story!"

Cinderella smiled. "All right," she said. "Once upon a time, there was a young prince who lived in a beautiful castle. He had everything that money could buy—fine clothes, jewels, paintings, and more. But something was missing. He didn't have anyone special to love. . . ."

She continued the story for a long time. Each time she tried to stop, the mice begged for more. After a while, they couldn't keep their eyes open anymore. It was just too late.

When the last mouse had fallen asleep, Cinderella tiptoed to her own bed and climbed in, still thinking about the bedtime story. Dreaming up tales made her forget her life of chores.

Gus began to snore. Cinderella giggled and pulled up her covers. She glanced once more at the clock on the castle tower. "Oh, my," she murmured sleepily. "If the mice had their way, I'd be telling tales until midnight!"

She snuggled against her pillow and yawned. "If only," she added sleepily, "some of my stories would come true. . . ."

The birds began to sing a lullaby, and soon Cinderella was fast asleep, dreaming that someday she'd live in a beautiful castle.

Lucky's Busy Afternoon

Perdita and Pongo looked over at their puppies, who were curled up together in a basket. The two Dalmatians were going to a neighborhood party with their human pets, Rodger and Anita. Pongo was very excited, but Perdita was worried. "We won't be gone long," he promised.

"I'm just not sure we should leave the puppies," Perdita replied. "Will Nanny be able to handle them by herself?"

Pongo smiled at his little Dalmatians. They were sound asleep. "What could possibly go wrong?" he asked. "The puppies are napping. Besides, Nanny can handle anything."

Perdita nodded
and followed Pongo
outside. He's right, she told
herself firmly—the puppies will
be absolutely fine. They'll probably just sleep all afternoon.

Before long, Rolly's paw hit Pepper's ear and woke him up.
Then Patch nudged Lucky. A few minutes later, all of the puppies
were awake. They yawned and stretched.

The smell of fresh summer air made them want to go outside.
"Let's get Nanny to take us for a walk!" Lucky suggested.

"That'd be fun!" cried Patch.

The puppies found a leash
nearby. Then they yipped as
loudly as they could and
waited for Nanny to
come over.

When Nanny heard the puppies barking, she went to them right away. "Oh, dear," she said as she looked into their big, hopeful eyes. "You look like you want to go outside."

The puppies scampered out of the basket eagerly. "I don't think Pongo and Perdita would mind if we went for a walk," she said.

Soon Nanny and the Dalmatians were on their way. "Let's go to the playground," Nanny said. "It's the perfect spot for pups to play."

When they arrived, Nanny unhooked the puppies' leashes. The Dalmatians began to run around. It was a beautiful day! Patch and Pepper dug a hole in the sandbox. Rolly found a rope to chew on.

Lucky spotted a pretty butterfly and chased it up a slide.

The butterfly stopped over a nearby wall, so Lucky jumped toward it. As it flew away again, Lucky barked. *Woof! Woof!*

His brothers and sisters didn't hear him because they were busy playing. They didn't notice when Lucky jumped down to the other side of the wall.

But Lucky didn't land on the ground. He had jumped onto the back of a fire truck! It started speeding down the road.

Woo! Woo! The sirens blared.

Woof! Woof! Lucky barked. "I'm a fire dog!"

Soon the truck pulled to a stop. The firefighters got a ladder and set it up next to a big tree.

A kitten was stuck in one of the branches. Lucky barked at it to come down, but it didn't understand. Lucky didn't want to make the kitten more nervous, so he jumped off the truck. It was time to return to the playground anyway.

On his way back, Lucky saw a little girl with curly red hair pushing a doll carriage. "A puppy!" she exclaimed. She reached down and picked him up. "You can be my new dolly," she said. Then she tied a bonnet to Lucky's head and dropped him into the carriage. "I'm going to keep you forever."

Grrr. Lucky growled. He did not like being a doll. Besides, he had to get back to his family!

Suddenly, the little girl spotted something on the ground. "A button!" she cried. She bent down to pick it up. Lucky knew there was no time to lose. He jumped out of the carriage and used his paws to get the bonnet off. Then he ran down the street as fast as he could. At the end of the block, Lucky cocked his ears.

He could hear barking!

He raced across the street. *Beep! Beep!* A horn honked at him. He jumped back, and a car went roaring by— right through a mud puddle. Dirty water splashed all over Lucky, but he ran on. When he finally made it to the playground, he was out of breath.

Inside the playground, Nanny was trying to count the puppies, but they wouldn't stay in one place.

Lucky barked as he scratched eagerly at the gate. *Woof! Woof!*

Nanny looked up. "Why, hello, little pup," she said to him. "Too bad you can't come with us, but you're not a Dalmatian. You should find your own family—I'm sure they're worried."

Lucky was confused, but then he caught sight of his reflection in a nearby puddle. He was covered with dirt. He looked like a Labrador puppy—no wonder Nanny hadn't recognized him!

Then he heard some children laughing. He followed the sound and saw them playing in a fountain.

That's perfect, Lucky thought. He ran over and jumped in.

The children giggled and chased him around. "Look, he has spots," one of them said.

Lucky knew he must be clean. He got out of the fountain and shook his wet fur. A man sitting on a nearby bench looked over and frowned.

Better get out of here! Lucky thought. He ran home as fast as he could. Nanny was outside the house, unhooking his brothers' and sisters' leashes.

"My goodness," she said as Lucky ran past her and into the house. "Where did you come from?"

Later, when Pongo and Perdita came home, they found Lucky curled up in the sleeping basket.

"You see?" Pongo whispered to Perdita. "They're all here. I told you nothing would go wrong. Lucky's even asleep again. He must have had a wonderful afternoon."

Peter Pan

To the Rescue!

One day, Peter Pan and his friends
were playing Follow the Leader. As
usual, Peter was the leader. Tinker Bell,
the Lost Boys, and John, Michael,

and Wendy Darling were following him around Never Land.
Before long, they came to a stream.

"Let's cross it the fun way!" Peter suggested.

He grabbed a rope, swung out over the water, and landed
on the other side. His friends followed, until only John was left.

"Tallyho!" John cried, and he leaped for the rope. He missed it and fell into the stream. *Splash!*

As Michael helped him out of the water, John grumbled, "Why does Peter always have to be in charge? Just once I'd like to do things my way!"

John decided he wanted to show Peter how brave and clever he was. A little farther down the trail, he had an idea. "By Jove," he cried, "I've got it!"

"Got what?" asked Michael.

John said, "You'll see." He took Michael's hand, and together they slipped off into the forest.

John and Michael disguised themselves as pirates, hopped in a small boat, and began to row toward a pirate ship in the harbor. But it wasn't just any ship—it was Captain Hook's! He and Peter Pan were sworn enemies.

"Where are we going?" asked Michael.

"To spy on Captain Hook!" John said excitedly. "We'll take the information back to Peter."

As the boys reached Hook's ship, they heard a noise. *Ticktock!*

"What's that?" asked Michael. Just then, a pair of beady eyes poked up out of the water. It was the Crocodile. Once, he'd swallowed an alarm clock, and now he always made a ticking sound.

"Be careful!" John warned.

John and Michael climbed over the side of the ship carefully. John spotted two mops and a bucket. He whispered to his brother, "Pretend you're washing the deck."

A moment later, Smee, the first mate, came around the corner. "Ahoy, mateys!" he called. "Can't say that I remember you. But whoever you are, you're doing a fine job!"

144

When Smee was gone, John turned to Michael and said,
"Come on, we've got some spying to do. I'm going to look for
Hook." He found a telescope and climbed up the rigging.

Smee walked by again. "Do you see anything?" he asked.

"Uh, a storm, actually!" John blurted out.

"I should tell the captain," Smee replied. He hurried off.

John turned to Michael. "This is perfect. He'll lead us right to Captain Hook!" They followed Smee at a safe distance and saw him enter a cabin. "Stand watch. I'll be right back," John whispered to his brother.

When John peered through the porthole of the cabin, he saw Captain Hook. Unfortunately, the pirate also saw him. Unlike Smee, Hook could tell that John was not a real pirate.

"Spies!" thundered Hook. "Get them, Smee!"

"We're doomed!" Michael cried.

"Not necessarily," said John.

The first mate came scuttling out of the cabin. When he saw the boys, he said, "Oh, it's you!"

"Indeed it is," said John. "We've been checking the safety of the captain's quarters, and I must say that we're shocked. Why, spies could look through that porthole as easily as I did!"

Smee led the boys inside. "What's the meaning of this?" Captain Hook demanded.

The first mate stammered, "Th-they said they were checking on your safety, sir. And I must say, they're hard workers. Just today I saw them swabbing the deck and standing lookout."

The captain looked John straight in the eye. "Yes," he agreed. "I think they're doing a fine job. After all, with the attack only three days away, security is more important than ever."

"Attack?" said John.

Hook said, "Yes, on Peter Pan's hideout." He turned to his first mate. "Release them, Smee. We've got work to do."

As soon as the boys were outside, John whispered to Michael, "We have to warn Peter!" Quickly, they climbed over the side of the ship and began rowing toward shore.

Captain Hook laughed as he watched through his telescope.

"They'll lead us straight to Pan!" he said.

Smee straightened his glasses and looked at Hook. "Y-you mean, they really *were* spies?"

"Of course," the pirate replied. "They're some of Pan's little friends. They don't know it yet, but now they are working for us!"

A short time later, John and Michael reached the shore. "My plan worked!" John cried. "Wait till Peter hears!"

"Uh-oh," Michael said. "I hear ticking. Like a clock. Like a clock in a crocodile. Like a clock in a crocodile that follows Captain Hook!"

The boys looked at each other. "Hook?" they said. "Run!"

They scrambled up a hill, with John leading the way. When John reached the top, he called, "This way, Michael!"

But there was no answer. . . .

"Michael?" John said, looking over his shoulder.

Captain Hook was standing at the bottom of the hill. Beside him, two pirates had Michael in their clutches.

"Keep going, John!" cried Michael. "Don't stop!"

A few minutes later, John burst into Peter's hideout. "Come quick!" he yelled. Peter, Wendy, and the others gathered around him. John told them what had happened to Michael and that Hook was planning to attack.

Peter shook his head. "If Hook knew where I lived, why would he have followed you? I think it was a trick."

"He knew Michael and I weren't pirates?" asked John.

"I'm afraid so," Peter said.

John groaned. "I've made a terrible mess of things. Will you help?"

"Sure. I've got a plan," Peter replied. "Let's go!"

On the pirate ship, Smee tied Michael to a chair, while Hook tried to find out where the secret entrance to Peter's hideout was.

Just then, they heard a girl's voice say, "Captain Hook?"

It was Wendy. She was standing on the ship's plank. "Watch the boy, Smee," Hook said. "I'll be right back!"

As soon as Hook was gone, John looked into the porthole.

"Not you again!" Smee exclaimed and chased after John.

The Lost Boys hurried inside and untied Michael. Then they climbed down into a boat that was waiting below.

When the boys were all safe, John opened his umbrella, leaped over the side of the ship, and floated down to join them. Then the Lost Boys cast off and headed for shore.

Meanwhile, on the ship's plank, Captain Hook reached out to grab Wendy. Suddenly, a green blur streaked through the air and scooped her up. It was Peter Pan!

"Blast you, Pan!" Hook cried. He lunged forward and fell overboard, snagging the plank with his hook. "Smee!" Hook cried as the Crocodile circled below.

Later that evening, Peter and his friends sat in their hideout, talking about the rescue.

"When Michael and I met Captain Hook, how did he know we weren't pirates?" asked John.

"Pirates don't usually carry umbrellas," Peter said, smiling.

Everyone laughed. What an adventure they'd had!

FINDING NEMO

The Surprise Party

One day, Nemo, a little clown fish, was telling his dad, Marlin, about something their good friend Dory had done.

"You know," said Marlin, "Dory's birthday is coming up. She mentioned it a while ago. But I'm sure she's probably forgotten all about it."

Nemo decided he wanted to do something special for Dory. After all, she was like family. I know, he thought, I'll throw her a surprise birthday party!

At recess the next day, Nemo asked his friends Pearl the octopus, Tad the butterfly fish, and Sheldon the sea horse to help plan Dory's party.

"Count me in," said Pearl.

"Me, too," Sheldon agreed.

"I love parties!" Tad exclaimed.

"Then let's meet right after school and start planning," Nemo suggested.

That afternoon, the friends met near the sponge beds. Soon they were having a contest to see who could bounce the highest. After they declared Pearl the winner, they got down to work.

"What kind of food should we have at Dory's party?" asked Nemo.

"Kelp cake and algae ice cream," Sheldon replied.

"What about sea-plant pizza?" asked Tad. "And salty seawater punch?"

"I'm getting hungry already," said Nemo. "Now what should we do about music? I wish we knew a band."

"*We* could be the band," said Pearl. "I'm great on the sand-dollar tambourines."

"Yeah, and I play the clamshell drums," said Sheldon.

"Great!" cried Nemo. "And Tad can strum some kelp while I play the conch shell. Let's meet here tomorrow after school to practice."

Back at home that evening, Nemo told Marlin about the party.

Marlin looked a little worried for a moment. Then he reminded himself how clever Nemo was. He smiled at his son. "That's a big project," he said. "But if you put your mind to it, I'm sure you can do it."

"I can, Dad!" Nemo said confidently. "Dory's surprise party is going to be the best ever. Just wait and see."

The next day, Nemo and his friends were swimming toward the sponge beds with their musical instruments when they bumped into Dory.

"Hi Mimo! Hi kids!" Dory exclaimed. She had trouble remembering anything, especially Nemo's name. "What are you up to?"

"Er . . . umm," Nemo stammered.

"Music-class homework," Tad piped up.

"Well, have fun," said Dory, swimming off in the other direction.

The friends smiled at each other and began to practice. At first, they didn't sound very good. But after a while, they began to hit their groove.

163

After school the next afternoon, Nemo and his friends talked about who to invite to the party.

"What about Crush and Squirt?" Sheldon suggested. "Sea turtles sure know how to have a good time."

"Everyone from school, including Mr. Ray," said Tad.

"And I'll invite Bruce, Anchor, and Chum," Nemo said. "They may be sharks, but they're friends of Dory's."

"Let's give them a job so they stay out of trouble," said Pearl. "Like serving the punch. Okay, I think we're all set."

Tad, Pearl, Sheldon, and Nemo swam off to invite the guests.

Finally, it was the day of the party! Nemo and his friends woke up early and started decorating. Pearl talked some starfish into making a pretty pattern on a large piece of coral. Tad and Sheldon strung seaweed streamers. Then Nemo suggested they practice singing "Happy Birthday."

Just as they finished the last line, they heard another voice join in. It was Dory!

"I love singing!" she exclaimed. "How did you know it was my birthday?"

"You told me," said Nemo.

"Really, Nano?" asked Dory. "I don't remember that."

"Now the surprise is ruined," said Nemo sadly.

"What?" said Dory. "Someone ruined your surprise? Just tell me who did it. I'll fix things."

"You mean you've forgotten already?" asked Nemo.

"Forgotten what?" Dory replied.

"Nothing," said Nemo, cracking a smile. It sure was helpful that Dory's memory wasn't very good.

"See you later," said Dory, swimming away. "Who was that birthday fish anyway?" she muttered to herself. "I think it was someone really nice, someone I really liked. . . ."

"Another close call," said Nemo to his friends. "But I think we're all set. Why don't we go home and get ready? I'll meet you guys back here with Dory."

"Nemo, I don't know if I can come to the party," said Sheldon. "My dad wants me to watch the babies."

"Bring them along," said Nemo. "The more, the merrier."

A few hours later, the guests arrived. They all hid and waited to surprise Dory. When Dory and Nemo swam in, everyone popped out of their hiding places and shouted, "Surprise!"

"Look, Pluto, it's a party for you!" Dory cried.

"No, Dory, it's for *you*," Nemo said. "It's your birthday."

"It is?" asked Dory. "Oh, yeah. Cool! A party for me!"

The guests cheered. Dory smiled and blushed.

Nemo led everyone in singing "Happy Birthday." Dory joined in and sang the loudest.

"You're the best friends a fish could have," said Dory. Later, she swam over to Marlin and Nemo. "I sure am glad your dad and I found you, Nemo. This is the best birthday I've ever had."

"Hey, Dory," said Nemo. "You remembered my name."

"What's that, Flipper?" asked Dory.

"Oh, nothing," Nemo said with a sigh. "Let's get some food."

"Salty seawater punch!" exclaimed Dory. "My favorite."

"Allow me to pour you some," said Bruce, the great white shark, as he flashed Dory a giant toothy grin.

"Why, thank you, sir," replied Dory.

"Happy birthday, Dory," said Chum. "You sure have a lot of food—I mean friends—here today."

"Fish are friends, not food," Anchor reminded the other two sharks.

"That's right, guys," said Dory. "Don't forget it. Hey, how about we all get some birthday cake?" They swam away.

The minute the sharks left, the other sea creatures swam over to get some punch.

Right about then, Nemo and his friends played their first song, which got everyone dancing. Even Marlin swayed a little to the melody. Later, Crush and his son Squirt whirled around to the music until they were so dizzy they had to take a break.

Crush saw Marlin and swam over to say hello. "Hey, good to see you. That son of yours is awesome, dude. This is a super party—and I've been to quite a few."

Dory couldn't remember any dance moves, so she just made them up as she went along. The sharks even shook a fin or two. Then Mr. Ray led everyone in a line dance. Nemo and the band took a break to join in.

Everyone had a lot of fun, but after a few hours it was time to go home. Nemo thanked Pearl, Tad, and Sheldon as they were leaving. "I couldn't have done it without you guys," he said.

"Boy," said Dory, "that birthday fish is lucky to have so many good friends."

"That lucky fish is you, Dory," Nemo reminded her.

"Oh, right, Mimo," Dory replied. "My memory just isn't very good. I think it's getting worse as I get older—or is it getting better? I can't remember. Anyway, let me thank you before I forget. This is the best birthday I've ever had." Then Dory swam on her way.

"You did a great job with Dory's surprise birthday party," Marlin told Nemo. "I'm proud of you."

"Thanks, Dad," said Nemo. "I was thinking we should start planning my birthday party. It's only nine months away. Have you worked on the guest list yet?"

Marlin smiled.

"Could we have a seaweed cake? It's the best kind. What do you think, Dad?" asked Nemo.

"Son," said Marlin. "If you're planning it, I'm sure your birthday party will be the best one ever."

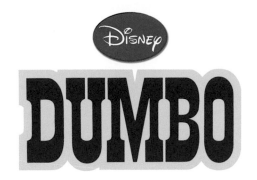

DUMBO

A Brand-New Act

Camels, horses, elephants, and bears stepped out of the circus train as it pulled into town. The big-top tent went up, and performers began to practice. Everyone was busy getting ready for the circus's first show.

Everyone, that is, except Dumbo the Flying Elephant. He just watched quietly.

"Hey, Dumbo, why so glum?" Timothy Mouse asked. He paused. "Oh, I know," he said. "You're tired of your act, aren't you? I suppose you want to try something new—something more exciting."

Dumbo nodded. He and Timothy stepped into the tent. They saw pretty white horses rehearsing their act. Dumbo loved watching the horses prance around the ring in their fancy headdresses and saddles.

"I think you'd be good at this," Timothy told his elephant friend. "You could be Dumbo the Elegant Elephant."

Timothy fastened a saddle and a bridle and feather onto Dumbo. "Now just keep your head up," he instructed. "You'll be great."

Dumbo stepped into the ring with the horses.

The circus monkeys had followed Dumbo into the tent. They thought the elephant looked silly marching with the horses, so they started giggling. *Hee, hee, hee!*

Dumbo didn't pay any attention to them. He just focused on the act. But after a few minutes, he tripped over his ears and fell. The elephant looked at Timothy Mouse and shrugged.

"Don't worry, Dumbo," the mouse said. "We'll find a new act that's more your style."

The two friends went back to another ring inside the tent and watched the trapeze artists swing above them.

"Your ears won't get in the way here!" Timothy exclaimed. "Dumbo the Acrobatic Elephant has a nice ring to it!"

After the performers were done, Dumbo flew to the platform and grabbed a trapeze.

"One, two, three—*go!*" Timothy shouted.

As Dumbo swung through the air, Timothy pushed a second trapeze toward him.

The little elephant caught it with his trunk. But now he was stuck in midair, holding two trapezes that swung from opposite sides of the ring!

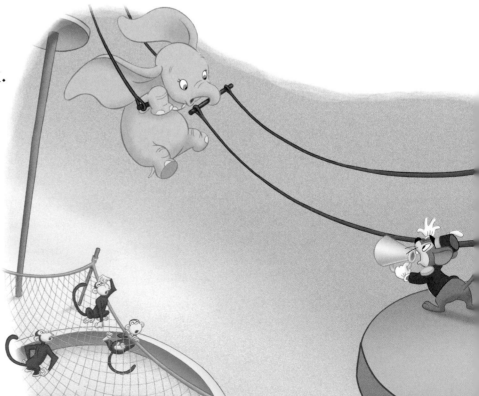

"Let go of one trapeze!" Timothy yelled.

But Dumbo couldn't hear.

"Let go!" the mouse repeated.

Dumbo let go of both trapezes at the same time! He fell toward the net below. When he landed, the net sank way, way down. Then—*whoosh!*—Dumbo bounced way, way up and sailed toward the top of the tent.

The monkeys shrieked with laughter.

When Dumbo reached the top of the tent, he began to fly!

"Way to go!" Timothy called as the elephant flew toward him. The monkeys cheered.

A few minutes later, Dumbo spotted the bear family entering the ring.

The youngest bear was learning a new act, too. He was trying to roll a barrel while balancing on it.

It wasn't easy, but at last he succeeded!

Then, Timothy and Dumbo watched as the entire bear family rehearsed their act. The bears juggled while they rode unicycles! It looked like lots of fun!

Timothy stroked his chin thoughtfully. "I bet you could do this. You could be Dumbo the Balancing Elephant!"

So Dumbo hopped on a unicycle. At first, he was a little wobbly. Then, he got his balance and began to pedal.

Dumbo rode proudly across the ring. But he was so excited that he forgot to watch where he was going. He was headed straight toward the snack bar!

"Dumbo! Look out!" Timothy shouted.

Dumbo didn't know how to stop, though. *Bam!* The unicycle hit the side of the ring.

The little elephant sailed through the air and landed in the snack bar with a crash!

Dumbo wasn't hurt, but he was covered in cotton candy!

"Oh, dear," Timothy fussed, trying to wipe off the mess. "You need a good bath. Hurry—it's almost showtime."

Dumbo went to clean up in a tub just outside the tent. The band began to rehearse, and one of the monkeys stuck a banana in a tuba.

When the tuba player blew a note, the banana flew out, and another monkey caught it.

Dumbo and Timothy saw what had happened and couldn't stop laughing. Then the little elephant had an idea.

When the band left to change into their uniforms, Dumbo filled his trunk with soapy water and poured it into the band's instruments.

The band returned shortly after and began to play as they marched into the circus ring.

With every note, bubbles poured out of the instruments. The audience went crazy!

Then Dumbo filled his trunk with soapy water again and flew into the circus ring.

The audience cheered wildly as he soared over them. He blew bubbles until the circus tent was filled with them. Everyone loved the act. They clapped and waved and tried to catch the bubbles.

"Wow!" Timothy exclaimed when Dumbo's performance was over. "You're Dumbo the Flying Elephant—with Bubbles! I think you've finally found an act that's just your style!"

Dumbo smiled happily. It was a great way to end the day.

A Day with Papa

Thumper was terribly excited. He and his dad were spending the day together, just the two of them. "Papa and I are going to have some great adventures in the forest," he told his sisters.

Thumper wondered what Papa had planned. Maybe they would climb a mountain . . . or explore a cave together.

"I thought we'd gather some greens for supper," Papa Bunny said. "Remember, eating greens is a special treat. It makes long ears—and great big feet!"

"Yes, Papa," said Thumper, his heart sinking.

Thumper and Papa got straight to work.

A little while later, Thumper wanted a nice, cool drink. After all, he'd been picking leaves for at least an hour.

"Don't dawdle," said Papa Bunny.

"I won't, Papa," replied Thumper. And off he went.

While Thumper had some water, he saw ducks splashing
near a waterfall. He wished he could join them. But he knew
that Papa was waiting. So he kept on going.

Thumper hadn't hopped very far when he saw the frogs playing. *Ribbit, ribbit!* That sure seemed like fun!

Then Thumper remembered Papa, hard at work.

After a few more hops, Thumper saw his friend the opossum.

"Want to climb this tree with me?" the opossum asked.

"Okay!" Thumper said, forgetting about his papa. With a little boost from his friend, Thumper was soon exploring the old oak tree. The two peered into a bird's nest. *Chirp, chirp!*

They woke up a sleepy owl. *Whooooooooo!*

They got close, but not *too* close, to a buzzing beehive. *Bzzz, bzzz.*

200

"Well, it's time for me to go," the opossum said
after a while. "My father is waiting for me."

Uh-oh! Thumper remembered his own papa.

He looked down at the ground. It was very far away, much
further than he remembered. How would he ever get down?

As Thumper waited, a little squirrel came by. "Well, hello there, Thumper," she said. "Why don't you use your claws to get down?"

But Thumper didn't have claws.

Thumper sighed. "Only one person can help me," he said.

"*Whooo?*" asked the owl.

"My papa," said Thumper sadly.

"I thought you'd never ask!" said a voice from down below.
"I've been looking for you everywhere."

"Papa?" Thumper asked hopefully.

"Yes, Thumper, it's me," Papa Bunny replied. "Now take a
deep breath and look down."

Thumper opened one eye. His papa was reaching for him.

The ground looked a lot closer now. Thumper reached down and his father pulled him tight.

"You must never be afraid to ask me for help. I am your father, and I will always be here for you," Papa Bunny said.

"I know, Papa," said Thumper.

"Well, all work and no play makes for a bored little bunny!" said Papa. "Why don't we race back to the meadow? Then we'll explore a hidden cave. The last one there is a slowpoke!"

That night, the bunnies ate fresh greens. Everyone agreed they were oh-so-tasty.

"Did you have lots of adventures?" Tessie asked.

"Why, yes," boasted Thumper. "I even climbed a tree!"

"Oh, my," said Daisy. "Were you scared?"

"What a silly question," Trixie scoffed. "Thumper is never scared."

Thumper looked at his dad, who gave him a big wink. Thumper grinned. He was glad he'd gotten to spend the day with his papa.

Pinocchio
A Nose for Trouble

School was out for the day, and Pinocchio was ready to have some fun. The puppet skipped down the cobblestoned street.

A small figure followed him, clutching an umbrella. It was Pinocchio's pal, Jiminy Cricket. "Wait for me!" he called.

Jiminy caught up with Pinocchio in front of the small shop where the puppet lived with Geppetto, his father. Geppetto carved all sorts of things out of wood—but his greatest creation was Pinocchio. The night he'd finished carving Pinocchio, he'd wished the puppet were a real boy. Then the Blue Fairy appeared and brought Pinocchio to life. If the puppet proved himself worthy, someday he'd become a real boy.

"Father, I'm home!" Pinocchio called. The only answer was the ticktock of a dozen clocks.

"Father?" Pinocchio said. He went into the next room and found Geppetto seated at a workbench.

"What are you making?" Pinocchio asked.

"A cuckoo clock," Geppetto replied. "I even brought home a live bird for a model. That way I can carve the cuckoo just right." He pointed to a birdcage.

"May I take the bird out and play with him?" Pinocchio asked excitedly.

"I'm afraid not," said Geppetto. "You aren't the only one who's been watching him."

Geppetto nodded toward Figaro the cat, who was following the cuckoo's every move.

"Please?" begged Pinocchio. "I'll be careful."

"I'm sorry, son," Geppetto said gently. "I wouldn't want Figaro to chase him."

Pinocchio spent the afternoon in the workshop. Every few minutes he glanced up at the birdcage and imagined what fun it would be to have the cuckoo perch on his finger. Pinocchio had never held a live bird before, and he was very curious to find out if it would sing to him. Would it sit on his shoulder and go wherever he went? he wondered.

At the end of the day, Geppetto went out to the market. As soon as he left, Pinocchio hurried over to the birdcage.

"Pinocchio?" Jiminy said. "What are you doing?"

"Taking the bird out so we can visit," the puppet replied. "Don't worry."

As Pinocchio opened the cage door, Figaro jumped onto the table.

"Watch out!" Jiminy cried as the cat leaped toward the open birdcage.

Figaro was fast, but the cuckoo was faster. The bird zipped out of the cage.

215

Crash! Figaro hit the side of the cage.

The cuckoo flew around the room. "See?" Pinocchio told Jiminy. "I told you it would be fine."

"I don't know," the cricket murmured. "You shouldn't have disobeyed your father." The cuckoo darted in and out of the rafters, then began to investigate Geppetto's clocks. Wherever the bird went, Figaro followed him.

Jiminy climbed onto the windowsill to get a better view. All of a sudden, the cuckoo turned and began flying straight toward him!

"Look out!" cried Pinocchio.

Jiminy leaped to one side.

The cuckoo had just spotted an open window. With a happy cry, he flew past Jiminy and out of the shop.

Just then, Geppetto walked in. He glanced at the empty birdcage. "Pinocchio!" he yelled. "I told you not to open the cage! Now look what has happened! I'm very disappointed."

Pinocchio looked around the room and spotted Figaro. "I didn't do it," he lied. "It was Figaro. He opened the birdcage and ate the cuckoo."

"Figaro!" cried Geppetto.

He picked up the cat to scold him, which was lucky for Pinocchio, because at that moment the puppet's nose began to grow. It inched out farther and farther, until it was the length of a crayon. It was growing because he had lied. Pinocchio didn't want his father to realize he had told a lie. So he tried to hide his nose.

"Father," Pinocchio said, "I think I'll go to bed early tonight. I'm not feeling well."

By the time Pinocchio had gotten under the covers, his nose had grown another inch.

The next morning, Pinocchio sneaked out of bed early. Then he headed for the door, calling, "Good-bye, Father! I'm off to school!"

Jiminy hurried after him. He knew Pinocchio wasn't going to school, because his nose was growing again.

"Pinocchio," Jiminy said, "you must start telling the truth."

"I can't!" cried Pinocchio. "I'll get into too much trouble."

Pinocchio hurried through the village, asking people if they'd seen the cuckoo. Then he climbed the bell tower and looked out across the sky. Next he bought a birdhouse and some seeds, hoping the cuckoo would stop by for a snack. But he didn't have any luck.

Wherever Pinocchio went, Jiminy Cricket followed along, trying to convince him to tell the truth. But Pinocchio wouldn't listen.

Pinocchio told lie after lie—about why he wasn't at school, where he was going, and what he was doing. Each time, his nose grew a little longer.

At the end of the day, Pinocchio's nose was longer than ever before—and he still hadn't found the cuckoo.

"Maybe you're right," Pinocchio said with a sigh. "It's time to tell the truth."

The puppet began to walk back through the streets of the village. Jiminy had to run ahead to clear a path. At last they got home, with Pinocchio arriving several seconds after Jiminy and his nose.

"Figaro didn't really eat the cuckoo," Pinocchio told his father. "I opened the birdcage, and the cuckoo flew away. I'm sorry I disobeyed you, but most of all, I'm sorry I lied."

As Pinocchio spoke, his nose became shorter and shorter, until it was back to its normal size.

"I'm glad you finally told the truth," said Geppetto. "And now I have something to show you."

He led Pinocchio inside, where an object sat on the table covered with a sheet. Had his father finished carving the clock? Geppetto drew aside the sheet, and under it was a birdcage—with the cuckoo inside!

"Where did you find him?" Pinocchio asked.

"I was working on the clock today, and he flew in through the window. I think he likes it here!" Geppetto exclaimed.

"He should," Pinocchio said. "It's the best home anyone could ever want."

Before long, night had fallen. Pinocchio yawned. "I think it's time for bed," Geppetto said with a smile.

Pinocchio gave his father a hug and got into bed. The cuckoo sang sweetly, and everyone drifted off to sleep.

The Coziest Carriage

One day, O'Malley and Duchess took the kittens to visit their dear friend Scat Cat. O'Malley had lived in the same neighborhood as Scat Cat back when they were both alley cats.

But then O'Malley had met Duchess and her kittens, Berlioz, Toulouse, and Marie. He'd liked them so much he'd decided to become part of their family. They all lived in a grand mansion with their owner, Madame Bonfamille. Even though he'd moved, O'Malley liked to go visit his old pals.

Scat Cat lived in a junkyard, in a broken-down carriage that had once been very grand. Now the spokes on the wheels were damaged, and there was an enormous hole in the roof.

Still, as far as Scat Cat was concerned, it could not have been more perfect. "I feel free here," he told the kittens. "I can come and go as I please. And when I stretch out on the cushions at night, I look up and there are the stars a-twinklin' back at me!"

The kittens had a grand time playing with Scat Cat in the junkyard. But when the sun went down, they were glad to return to the soft pillows, cozy blankets, and warm milk at Madame Bonfamille's.

A few days later, Scat Cat appeared at Madame's doorstep.

"My carriage is missing!" he explained to his friends. "I went into town to stretch my legs, and when I got back— *poof!*—the carriage was gone!"

"You will have to stay with us," said Duchess. "I'm sure Madame would be delighted to have you as our guest."

"Oh, goody!" the kittens cheered.

"You'll love it here," said Berlioz.

"Well," Scat Cat said, thinking it over, "that's a mighty nice invitation. Don't mind if I do." He plopped into an armchair. "Huh, no ripped cushions here!"

The kittens scampered up next to him. "Of course not," Marie said. "Madame would never allow worn-out chairs in her house. Only the best furniture will do."

Scat Cat nodded. "I guess everyone just has a different idea of what 'best' is, little lady. Me, I prefer cushions with the stuffing coming out of them. But who knows, maybe I'll get used to this."

"Would you like to paint with me?" Toulouse asked.

"How about I play a little piano music?" volunteered Berlioz.

"Or you could sing with me," Marie offered.

"Now, now, children," Duchess said. "Scat Cat just arrived. Let him settle in a bit."

But after just one night, Scat Cat didn't know if he *would* settle in. The life of a house cat just wasn't for him.

Everything at Madame Bonfamille's happened on a schedule. Meals were at eight o'clock, noon, and six o'clock, sharp. Naps were from nine to eleven, and one to four. Outings took place at 4:30. The rest of the time was spent in the house or in Madame's small, walled garden. The old cat was used to coming and going as he pleased.

"Do you know what I miss most?" Scat Cat said with a sigh. "My old carriage. What I wouldn't give to be able to look up at the sky and count the twinklin' stars as I drift off to sleep on those lumpy, worn-out cushions. . . ."

It was hard for the kittens to imagine how any cat could like a broken-down carriage better than a soft, cozy bed. But that's what Scat Cat had come to love, and that was good enough for them.

"I just wish there was some way we could get that carriage back for him," Marie said.

"Maybe there is!" Berlioz said with a grin. "Follow me!"

He led the kittens to the drawing room where their mother was relaxing.

"Can we go to the carriage house, Mama?" Berlioz asked.

"Well," their mother replied, "you are supposed to be practicing your Italian this afternoon."

"But it's for a special surprise for Scat Cat," Toulouse said.

"All right, then," Duchess said, "but just for a while."

237

A few minutes later, the kittens were inside Madame's carriage house. For some time now, Madame had been complaining about her old carriage. "It's not even worth repairing," she had said one day.

With this in mind, Berlioz climbed into the carriage and pounced on the old upholstery.

"Come on—dig in!" he said gleefully.

Toulouse and Marie joined him, and in no time the kittens had those cushions looking like the ones in Scat Cat's old carriage.

"Don't forget the roof!" Marie reminded her brothers. The kittens raced up to the top of the carriage, where they jumped and bounced. After a triple-backward somersault, Toulouse crashed through the carriage roof, making a huge hole.

"Hooray!" cheered Marie.

Just then, Madame walked in. She looked at the carriage. "It looks worse than I remember. Take it away at once."

That evening, the kittens got permission to take Scat Cat to the junkyard. "I don't believe it!" Scat Cat exclaimed when they showed him his new home. "It's even more torn up than my old carriage. It's *purr-fect!* How can I ever thank you?"

240

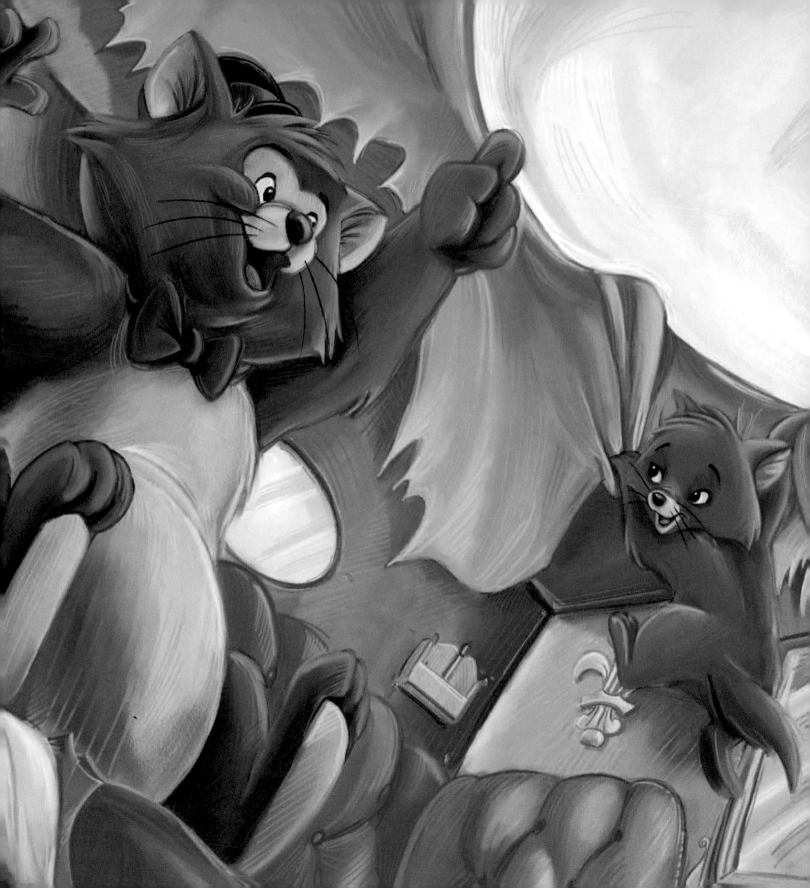

"Just promise you'll come back to visit us again," Berlioz told him. "And maybe have a little warm milk on hand when we come to see you."

"It's a deal," Scat Cat replied.

The kittens visited with their friend until the moon began to rise. Then they waved good-bye and headed home to snuggle beneath their cozy blankets.

In his new carriage, Scat Cat looked at the stars and smiled contentedly before drifting off to sleep.

Disney
Winnie the Pooh
Best-Friend Sleepover

"Comfortable, Piglet?" Winnie the Pooh asked as he tucked his friend into a drawer he had made into a bed.

"Oh, yes, Pooh. Thank you ever so much," Piglet replied. "The bed is just the right size."

"Well, good night, then," the bear said, blowing out the candle and climbing into bed.

"Good night, Pooh Bear," Piglet replied. He and Pooh were having a best-friend sleepover. It had been lots of fun so far. First, they had enjoyed a before-bedtime snack. Then, they had put on their pajamas and made up a story.

Of course, it was always fun spending time with Pooh. But there was something about being here for bedtime that was so . . . so . . . different from being at his own house, thought Piglet.

As he lay in the drawer, his eyes wide open, Piglet noticed that it seemed much darker here than it did at home.

"Pooh?" he called out softly. "Are you still awake?" He wanted to ask the bear if it was always so dark. When Pooh did not answer, Piglet realized that his friend must have fallen asleep.

Oh, well, Piglet thought as he rolled over and pulled up the covers. Then he closed his eyes tightly and tried to get to sleep.

After a while, Piglet peered out into the darkness. He hadn't been able to fall asleep yet. He noticed that it was very, very quiet in Pooh's room—much quieter than it was in Piglet's own room at night.

"Pooh? Pooh Bear?" Piglet called out, a little louder this time. He didn't want to wake up his friend. But he wondered if perhaps Pooh was awake and had just not heard him earlier.

Just then, the quiet was broken by a peculiar noise. Piglet sat up.

At first, the noise was a soft, low rumbling—curiously similar to the sound of a sleeping bear who was snoring. But Piglet thought a Heffalump was coming to get them.

"Pooh! Oh, d-d-dear!" Piglet shouted. He jumped out of the drawer and ran to his friend's bedside. He shook Pooh and shouted, "Wake up! Wake up! Oh, p-p-please, P-P-Pooh!"

"Hmm?" Pooh asked drowsily. Slowly, he climbed out of bed. He noticed Piglet wasn't in his drawer. Then he realized that Piglet was in his own bed!

"Listen to that horrible, horrible n-n-noise, Pooh," he stammered. Piglet listened for the noise so he could point it out to Pooh, then realized that it had stopped. "That's funny," said Piglet as he peeked out from under the covers. "The noise stopped as soon as you woke up."

"Hmm," the bear said, yawning. "I guess that means we can go back to sleep."

Piglet didn't think he'd be able to fall asleep.

"I don't mean to be a bad best friend," he said. "But do you think we might have the rest of our best-friend sleepover some other night? I'm just not used to sleeping anywhere but my own house."

Pooh sat on the bed and put his arm around Piglet. "I understand," he said. "We can have the rest of our best-friend sleepover whenever you like." Pooh helped Piglet gather his things. Then, hand in hand, they walked through the Wood to Piglet's house.

"Here you are, Piglet," Pooh said as they entered. "Home, sweet home."

"Thank you so much for walking me here," Piglet replied. "I suppose you'll be needing to get home to bed now?"

Pooh thought for a moment. "Yes, but first I might sit down for a little rest." He eyed a comfortable chair. "Just for a few minutes."

While Piglet unpacked, Pooh sat down and put up his feet. Then he decided to rest his eyes, just for a moment. His eyelids felt awfully heavy.

By the time Piglet finished, Pooh was fast asleep. He was even making a soft, rumbling sound.

But in the comfort of Piglet's own house, it did not sound scary like a Heffalump. It just sounded like a sleeping bear who was snoring.

Piglet covered Pooh with a small blanket and slipped a pillow under his head. "Sweet dreams, Pooh Bear," he whispered.

Then Piglet climbed into his bed and very quickly drifted off to sleep.

Pooh and Piglet slept all night. The next morning, Piglet woke up and saw that his friend was still asleep. He woke up Pooh gently, and they had a yummy breakfast. It had been a wonderful best-friend sleepover, after all.

Aladdin

Abu Monkeys Around

Early one morning in Agrabah, the Genie went to the marketplace with Jasmine, Aladdin, and Abu. The monkey seemed to be in an extra-mischievous mood. He had already lost Aladdin's favorite hat, and it wasn't even lunchtime!

When they arrived at the market, Aladdin asked the Genie to help him keep an eye on Abu.

"Sure, Al," the Genie said. "Anything for you."

Just then, Aladdin spotted Abu over by a fruit stand. The monkey was trying to juggle three apples and a watermelon—all at the same time!

"Abu! No!" Aladdin yelled. But it was too late. The fruit went flying.

The fruit seller was very angry. "What a mess!" he cried.

Luckily, the Genie quickly cleaned up with a little magic.

But Abu had already scampered off down another aisle.

"Uh-oh," said the Genie, shaking his head, "I think it's going to be a very long day."

Jasmine continued to shop. The Genie looked for Abu, but couldn't find him.

"Hey, Al!" he said. "Have you seen him?"

But Aladdin had lost sight of the monkey, too.

The Genie caught up to the monkey at a stand where a merchant was selling bananas. Abu was grabbing the fruit and peeling each one as fast as he could. He threw the peels over his shoulder, littering the ground.

"Abu! Stop that!" the Genie shouted.

Just then, Rajah the tiger, followed by Jasmine and Aladdin, came looking for Abu. As they rounded the corner, they slipped on the peels lying on the ground!

"Whoa! Whoa! Whoops!" Aladdin and Jasmine lost their balance.

The Genie tried to catch his friends as they fell, but he slipped, too. They all landed in a heap. When Abu saw them, he laughed and laughed. But the Genie was not amused.

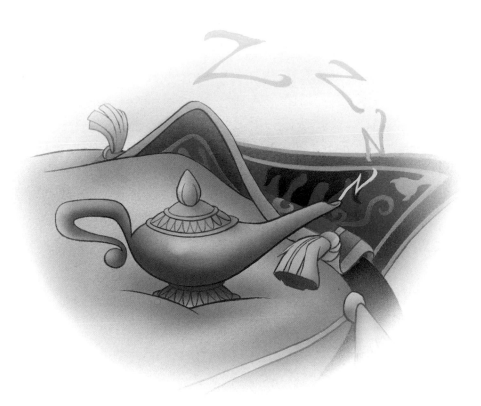

When it began to get dark at the market, the group returned to the palace. The Genie stretched and yawned. He had been chasing Abu all day, and now he was ready to take a rest inside his lamp.

"Good night, Abu," he told the monkey. "I'll see you in the morning."

Abu chattered loudly for a minute and then curled up on a fluffy pillow. He closed his eyes, but he couldn't sleep. Abu wanted to play with his friend the Genie. And he had thought of a way to wake him.

Abu swung a hammer and banged it against the lamp. *Clang!*

The Genie sprang out of the lamp. "*Goooooood* morning! Is it time to get up already? I feel as though I just went to sleep!" He looked out the window and saw that it was still dark. "Wait a minute, I *did* just go to sleep. Why am I awake?"

The Genie turned around and spotted Abu in the corner. "Abu, why are you holding a hammer?"

The monkey shrugged and smiled.

"This is *not* playtime," the Genie scolded. "It's nighty-night time. Genies need their beauty sleep. It's hard to look this fabulous all the time without it. Now go to bed!"

Abu nodded.

The Genie looked at him. "Good night, then."

After the Genie tucked himself into his lamp again, Abu still didn't feel like sleeping. Instead, the monkey tried to wake Aladdin to play with him. That didn't work. Then Abu woke up Jasmine to play. That *really* didn't work. Rajah roared and quickly scared Abu away!

The Genie got back to sleep, and before he knew it a bell was ringing. This time the Genie was up for good.

Abu swung across the hallway on a rope. Unfortunately, it was attached to a potted plant, which fell to the floor. *Crash!* Next Abu climbed up onto a mirror and made faces at himself. But he accidentally knocked the mirror to the ground. *Smash!* Then Abu rang the bell. *Clang! Clang! Clang!*

Finally, the Genie caught him. "Abu, you are keeping everyone up. It's time for sleep!" he shouted. "Now!"

Abu hung his head and scurried off to bed.

The following morning, no one at the palace could stop yawning. The Genie was so tired that his magic wasn't working well. Then Jasmine asked for a bunch of flowers, and instead the Genie's magic produced a bag of flour. When Aladdin asked for a storage trunk, he got an elephant.

By the afternoon, the Genie could hardly keep his eyes open. He sat down on the fountain edge in the garden. A moment later, he fell asleep. Next to him, Aladdin yawned, too. He had just drifted off to sleep when—

Splash! Abu jumped into the fountain. Water sprayed all over Aladdin, the Genie, and Rajah.

Abu chattered excitedly. Surely everyone would want to play with him now! Aladdin and the Genie looked at each other and smiled.

"Why not?" said Aladdin with a shrug. "Maybe this will tire out Abu."

The Genie agreed. After all, it *was* a hot day. He splashed Abu, and the monkey splashed him back. Then Aladdin, Jasmine, and Rajah joined in.

That night, Aladdin, Jasmine, and the Genie heard a strange sound. They followed it and found Abu fast asleep on a pillow.

"I guess all that monkeying around finally tired out Abu!" the Genie whispered, chuckling. He laid a blanket over Abu and stretched. "Well, I'm off to bed! Good night, Al. Good night, Jasmine," he told the prince and princess. "And good night, Abu—at last!"

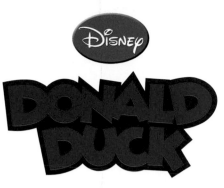

Donald Duck
Goes Camping

"Yippee!" Huey, Dewey, and Louie cried. They had just found out that their uncle, Donald Duck, was taking them camping.

Donald and his nephews began to load their gear into the car.

"I've got the tent and the food," Donald said.

"Here are the fishing poles," Huey said.

"Don't forget the sleeping bags," Louie reminded them.

"I'm bringing a camping guidebook," said Dewey. "There's all kinds of great information in here about wildlife. You never know—we might need it."

"You don't need a guidebook," Donald said confidently. "I know everything there is to know about camping."

Donald and his nephews hopped into the car and headed toward the forest. A couple of hours later, they arrived in the woods and found a camping spot.

Huey and Louie helped their uncle put up the tent while Dewey read the guidebook.

When they were finished setting up the tent, they put their food inside a wooden locker to keep it away from wild animals.

"The guidebook says to hang the food locker from a tree," said Dewey. "It says bears will eat almost *anything*!"

"I already told you, I know everything there is to know about camping," Donald said. "Animals aren't going to take food from me!"

Just then, two squirrels scampered down from a big oak tree and snatched a bag of peanuts.

"Hey!" Donald shouted as the squirrels scurried back up the tree. "Come back here!"

"The guidebook says it's good to share with *little* animals," said Louie. "But we shouldn't try to share with bears!"

"I don't care what the book says. Those are *my* peanuts!" replied Donald. He grabbed an ax from the camping supplies.

With all his might, Donald swung the ax toward the base of the tree. *Crack!* He chopped a large hole in the tree trunk, and a stream of acorns spilled onto the ground.

"Why did you do that, Uncle Donald?" asked Dewey. "You spilled the squirrels' supply of acorns for the winter."

"They stole my peanuts," said Donald angrily.

The squirrels glared at Donald Duck and then darted away. Donald chuckled. "What silly little animals!"

A little while later, Huey looked up from his camping book. "Uh-oh!" he said, pointing into the woods. A large bear was charging toward them!

"Run!" Donald shouted. He and his nephews scrambled up some nearby trees. The bear came to a stop.

He had spotted the picnic table. He began to sniff at the food locker. The two squirrels had arrived with the bear, and they sat on a branch overlooking the campsite. With one swipe of his big paw, the bear broke open the food locker. Then he took a baked ham and left.

"The guidebook was right," said Huey. "We should have hung the locker from a tree."

Donald climbed down to the ground. "I don't need a book to tell me what to do!" he said, annoyed.

The two squirrels ran along the tree branches and chattered at Donald again. This time, they seemed to be laughing at him.

"I'll get even with you!" Donald yelled. He climbed toward the squirrels. Just as he was about to grab them, they leaped onto a thin branch that was high above the river.

"I've got you now," said Donald. He crawled out onto the branch.

"Unca Donald!" Dewey shouted. "The book says to stay off small branches!"

Crrrrack! Suddenly, the branch broke, and Donald fell into the river.

The water swiftly carried him downstream. His nephews ran alongside him. Soon they heard the thundering sound of a waterfall.

"Help!" Donald cried. "Pull me out!" He tried to swim toward the riverbank, but the current was too strong.

Up in the trees, the squirrels chattered gleefully.

"Shame on you!" Louie scolded the squirrels. "How would you feel if your uncle was headed toward a waterfall?" The squirrels stopped laughing and darted into the underbrush.

In the river, Donald spotted a big rock and grabbed on to it.

"Do something!" he called to his nephews. "Anything! Look in the guidebook!"

Huey, Dewey, and Louie started flipping through the camping guide, searching for a way to help their uncle. They only looked up when the squirrels returned—with a brown beaver!

The beaver waddled to a tree that stood beside the river and began to gnaw at it.

"What's he doing?" asked Louie.

"He's trying to help!" Dewey replied. "If the tree falls into the river, it might be long enough to reach Uncle Donald. Please hurry!"

A few minutes later, the tree fell over with a crash. It landed next to the rock that Donald was clinging to.

Donald crept along the tree trunk toward dry land. Soon he was safely ashore. Huey, Dewey, and Louie gave him a big hug.

"You made it!" Dewey exclaimed.

"Were you scared?" Louie asked.

"Don't worry, Uncle Donald," Huey said. "I would have thought of something."

Donald didn't answer. Instead, he ran toward his car.

"Where are you going?" his nephews called. "Aren't you going to thank the animals who rescued you?"

Donald just hopped in the car and sped away. Huey, Dewey, and Louie looked at each other and shrugged.

Donald returned in an hour. His car was filled with presents for the animals who had helped him. He had nuts for the squirrels, branches for the beaver, and a big bag of seeds for the birds.

The animals were delighted and began to munch on their treats.

Donald also had a sack of cement and a trowel.

"What's that for?" Louie asked.

"You'll see," said Donald.

He mixed the cement into a thick paste, and spread it with the trowel over the hole in the squirrels' big oak tree.

Donald's nephews watched him patch the hole. "Do you really know how to fix trees?" asked Huey.

"I do now," Donald said sheepishly. "I read all about it in the camping guidebook. You can learn a lot from books, you know!"

Mater in Paris

One lazy afternoon, Mater and Lizzie were listening to the radio. Suddenly the music stopped, and a voice spoke to Mater through the speakers. It was British secret agent Holley Shiftwell!

"Hello, Mater! Sorry to startle you. Finn and I are in Paris trying to track down several Lemon suspects from the World Grand Prix. We could use your help! Will you come join the mission?"

Mater was stunned. "Uh . . . sure thing! You can count on me, Holley!"

"Thank you, Mater!" said Holley. "Siddeley will pick you up and bring you to Paris straightaway."

The radio crackled and the music began playing again.

"Dadgum! Did you hear that, Lizzie?" Mater asked.

"Hmm? Yes, such pretty music," Lizzie mumbled.

As Mater was leaving Lizzie's, Siddeley the spy jet landed on Main Street!

Mater's best friend, Lightning McQueen, drove up. "Mater, what's going on?" he asked.

"I'm going on a secret mission in Paris," whispered Mater. "Hey, you want to come, too?"

"Paris? Um . . . well . . . sure," said Lightning, still in shock.

"*Woooowheee!*" exclaimed Mater.

Lightning had never been on a spy jet before. He was amazed by all the controls and screens.

A computer gave Mater and Lightning some gadgets, including communicators.

"You're a real superspy now!" said Mater.

When they arrived in Paris, Mater and Lightning met Holley and Finn in a private airport lounge.

"If I was a Lemon, I'd get me some spare parts!" said Mater.

"Brilliant," said Finn. "Why don't you visit Tomber, while Holley and I head to the markets on the west side of Paris."

"If you find the Lemons contact us immediately," said Holley. "Good luck!"

Tomber was upset when Mater and Lightning met up with him. "I've been robbed!" he exclaimed.

He gave Mater a list of the stolen parts.

"Them dadgum Lemons was here already," said Mater.

As he and Lightning left the marketplace, they discovered a trail of spare parts.

"Hey, look at this! All the stolen parts are right here . . . the distributor caps, crankshafts, and pistons. Only the mufflers and exhaust manifolds are missing," said Mater.

He thought for a moment. "Hugos always need new parts for their rusty exhaust systems. We must be looking for Hugos!"

Mater and Lightning followed the spare parts all the way to Paris's most famous museum—the Louvre.

They cruised through the rooms of the museum looking for signs of the Hugos. Inside the Motor Lisa room, Lightning nearly drove through a puddle of oil.

"Ugh, somebody's leaking oil," said Lightning.

Mater's eyes widened. "Don't look at me! I never leak."

Lightning laughed. "I know it wasn't you, buddy," he said. "But whoever it was sure could use an oil change."

"You're right," said Mater. "This oil is burnt and grimy." He noticed tire tracks leading away from the puddle. "And these tread patterns match the ones on Hugo tires!"

Mater and Lightning followed the tire tracks to a nearby café. Mater noticed two cars with odd-looking luggage racks and front grilles. Suddenly, one of them backfired and the grille fell off. It was a disguise!

"Hugos!" gasped Mater. "Their rusty exhaust systems cause 'em to backfire!"

The Hugos became nervous and left the café. Mater and Lightning followed them to a dance hall called the Moteur Rouge.

Mater and Lightning went in after them and found themselves on the stage.

"We gotta blend in," said Mater, tossing Lightning some Car-Car–dancer feathers.

Mater and Lightning kicked up their tires and danced their way across the stage!

The spy duo followed the Hugos through an exit and into an alley.

"Uh-oh," said Mater.

There were not two, but six Hugo thugs surrounding them!

"We're getting rid of you once and for all, tow truck, and your race-car friend, too!" yelled the Hugos.

The Hugos tried to ram Lightning from the side, but Lightning was too quick.

Then the Hugos released knockout gas. But Mater spun his tow hook superfast to blow the gas back at the Hugos. The two thugs instantly passed out.

Mater and Lightning split up.

Mater called Holley. "We found the Lemons!"

"Well done!" said Holley. "Where are they?"

"Right behind me," Mater replied. "And they don't look happy."

"I'm locking onto your location now. Finn and I are on our way!" said Holley.

"Wait! I've got an idea," said Mater. "Meet us at the top of the Eiffel Tower." He then contacted Lightning.

Mater and Lightning raced to the top of the Eiffel Tower. Moments later the two Hugos reached the top, but they were so tired that they immediately tipped over and passed out.

"Good job, superspy buddy," Mater said to Lightning. "We wore them out!" He pointed to one of the Hugos. He had shiny new exhaust parts.

"Great job!" said Holley again. Finn nodded in agreement.

After the police towed the Hugos away, Lightning looked at Mater. "Ready for our next mission, buddy? The races at Le Motor!"

"*Wooohooo!*" exclaimed Mater. "Now you're talkin'!" The two best friends revved their engines and took off into the night.